COYOTE

A TRICKSTER TALE FROM THE AMERICAN SOUTHWEST

TOLD AND ILLUSTRATED BY

Gerald McDermott

Harcourt Brace & Company

San Diego   New York   London

Requests for permission to make copies of any part of the work should be
mailed to the following address: Permissions Department, Harcourt, Inc.,
6277 Sea Harbor Drive, Orlando, Florida 32887-6777.

Library of Congress Cataloging-in-Publication Data
McDermott, Gerald.
Coyote: a trickster tale from the Southwest/told and illustrated by
Gerald McDermott.—1st ed.
p.   cm.
Summary: Coyote, who has a nose for trouble, insists that the crows
teach him how to fly, but the experience ends in disaster for him.
1. Indians of North America—Southwest, New—Legends. 2. Coyote
(Legendary character)—Legends. [1. Coyote (Legendary character)
2. Indians of North America—Southwest, New—Legends.] I. Title.
E78.S7M136   1994
398.24'52974442—dc20
[E]   92-32979
ISBN 0-15-220724-4

The paintings in this book were done in gouache, colored pencil, and
pastel on heavyweight cold-press watercolor paper.
The display type and text type were set in Bryn Mawr by
Central Graphics, San Diego, California.
Color separations by Bright Arts, Ltd., Singapore
Printed and bound by Tien Wah Press, Singapore
This book was printed on totally chlorine-free Nymolla Matte Art paper.
Production supervision by Warren Wallerstein and David Hough
Typography designed by Lydia D'moch

Printed in Singapore

L K J I H G F E D C

Coyote stories are the most widely known and most
often told trickster tales of Native American tradi-
tion. From the Great Basin, to the Plains, to the
pueblos of the Southwest, Coyote's misadventures
have delighted and instructed for many centuries.
His very name, *coyotl*, derives from Nahuatl, the
ancient language of the Aztecs.

Stone Age hunters revered the coyote and tried to
emulate the animal's cleverness and endurance.
But for the Native American shepherds and planters
of later ages, the coyote's conniving and thievery
were a nuisance—and so he came to be mistrusted
and vilified.

Coyote's image as a troublesome trickster, espe-
cially among the tribes of the Southwest, emerges in
storytelling. He is portrayed as a devious, glut-
tonous fool, the perpetual victim of his own
inquisitiveness. Coyote's insatiable desire to imitate
others, to intrude on their lives, makes him seem
very foolish . . . and very human.

The people of the Pueblo of Zuni, who excel in
telling Coyote tales, assign a symbolic color to each
of the world directions. They associate Coyote with
the West and the color blue. In the present story—as
in many Zuni tales of Coyote—he serves as an exam-
ple of human vanity, and his misbehavior brings him
misfortune.

—G. M.

For Jaycee, Joshua, and Alec

Coyote.
Blue Coyote.
He was going along, following his nose.
He had a nose for trouble.

Coyote stuck his nose into Badger's hole but got bitten.

Coyote wanted to have a flaming red head like Woodpecker, but his fur caught fire.

Coyote went looking for Snake but only found trouble.

Coyote was always in trouble.

Coyote came to a place where
earth meets sky.
He heard laughing and singing.
He went up to take a look.

Coyote saw a flock of crows.
They were chanting.
They were dancing.

Then the birds spread their wings.
They flew through the air and circled the canyon.

"Oh, if only I could fly," said Coyote. "I would be the greatest coyote in all the world!"

Coyote called to the crows.
"Let me join you," he said.

"This foolish coyote wants to be like us,"
Old Man Crow said to his flock.
"Let's have some fun with him."

Old Man Crow turned one eye toward Coyote.
"You may dance with us," he said.

"Thank you! Thank you!" said Coyote.
"But I want to fly, too!"

"Maybe you can," said Old Man Crow.

Old Man Crow plucked a feather from his left wing.
He told his flock to do the same. They stuck the feathers in Coyote.
Coyote winced. His nose twitched.

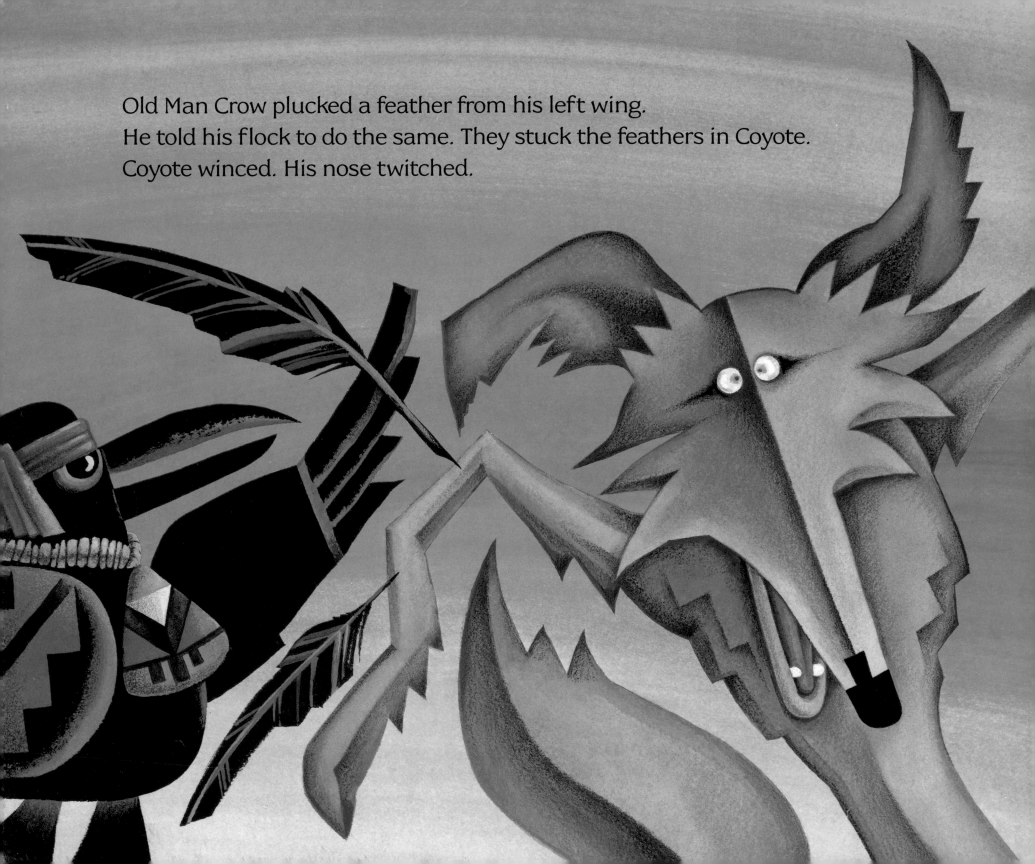

The crows chuckled.

"You are ready to fly," said Old Man Crow.

The birds began their slow, steady chant. They hopped from one foot to the other. Coyote joined in the dance. Even though he got out of step and sang out of tune, he was very proud of himself.

The crows spread their wings and soared
into the sky. Coyote followed. His flight
was jerky. He tilted to one side. Since his
feathers were only from the left wing of each
bird, he was off balance.

He fell to the ground.

"Wait!" he cried out.
"Don't leave me behind!"

The birds returned and gathered round Coyote.

"We must balance him," said Old Man Crow.

Old Man Crow plucked a feather from his *right* wing.
Each of his flock did the same. Coyote cringed as they stuck
the feathers in his fur. The crows cackled.

"Now I'm perfect!" said Coyote. "I can fly as well as the rest of you."

Coyote had become rude and boastful.
He danced out of step.
He sang off-key.
The crows were no longer having fun.

The birds again began their slow, steady chant.
Coyote hopped along, flapping his feathered legs and
singing sour notes.
The dancers spread their wings and leapt into the air.

Soon the crows were flying high over the canyon.
Coyote struggled to keep up.

"Carry me!" he demanded.

The crows circled Coyote but didn't carry him.
Instead, they took back their feathers, one by one.

Coyote sank through the air.

He fell straight down.

"Wooooooooooo!" he howled.

Coyote fell so fast, his tail caught fire.
He fell into a pool on the mesa.

Coyote crawled out of the water.
He heard laughter and saw the crows flying away.

Coyote ran after them.

He tripped and fell,
tumbling in the dirt.

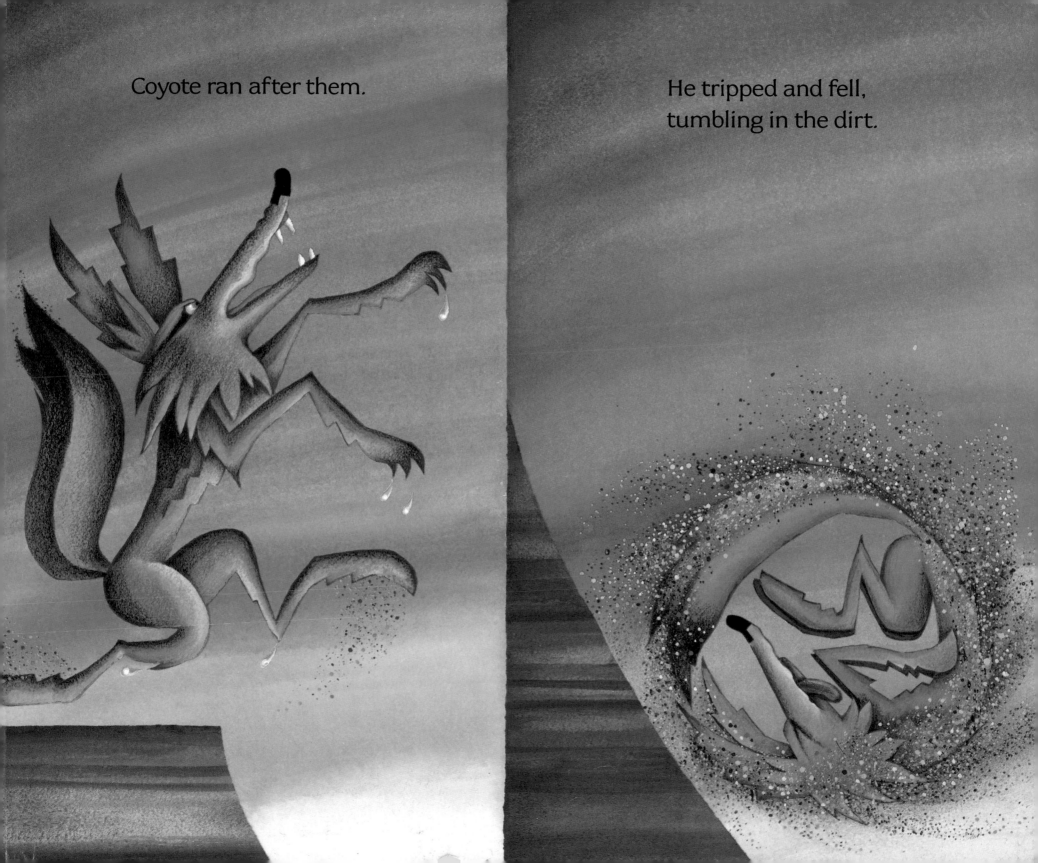

Coyote went home soaked and covered with dust.
To this day, he is the color of dust.
To this day, his tail has a burnt, black tip.

To this day, Coyote still follows his nose.
He has a nose for trouble.
He always finds it.